THE SOCIAL SEEKERS

E. L. Goodwin

authorHOUSE®

AuthorHouse™
1663 Liberty Drive
Bloomington, IN 47403
www.authorhouse.com
Phone: 1 (800) 839-8640

This is a work of fiction. All of the characters, names, incidents, organizations, and dialogue in this novel are either the products of the author's imagination or are used fictitiously.

Published by AuthorHouse   10/06/2015

ISBN: 978-1-5049-5451-8 (sc)
ISBN: 978-1-5049-5473-0 (e)

Library of Congress Control Number: 2015916414

Print information available on the last page.

Any people depicted in stock imagery provided by Thinkstock are models, and such images are being used for illustrative purposes only. Certain stock imagery © Thinkstock.

This book is printed on acid-free paper.

This book is dedicated to my Uncle Tom B. for his strength, courage, lightheartedness, inspiration, and love always. Also to recognize his endless love of reading an interesting book.

CONTENTS

CHAPTER 1

The Country Club Landscape

*I*n Shore Haven, it is unheard of to not belong to an elite country club. Between the country clubs, churches, benefits, dinner parties, scandals, and gossip, knowing how to navigate the social scene is essential. Maintaining and obtaining social status is required if you are in the social circle of Shore Haven's elite. It is just the way it is here. You have to belong to one club.

Numerous country clubs exist, and it is important to join the right one. Some are golf and tennis only. Others are sailing or field clubs. Still others are riding or equestrian clubs. At some, members play tennis and switch to paddle in the winter. At some, they come to watch polo matches, ride horses, or sit by the pool. At Shore Haven Country Club, they can do all of these activities and more because it is situated on the water and affords all luxuries with the exception of equestrian life. There is another club for that, if you want to join there too.

It is an exclusive world that comes at a price—not just financially but often socially as well. It can be socially rewarding or socially damaging, depending upon which club you join and with whom you associate. You have to know who your friends are—or who you think they are.

"Shore Haven Country Club is the right one for us," Ally Bennet explains to her husband, Todd, as they walk out of the club and back to their car, looking around.

"Well, the paperwork is in, and the Hunters are going to sponsor us," Todd replies, pleased to be officially playing golf there soon as a real member. Setting up tee times with sponsors becomes complicated at times.

To become an elite member, everyone has to be sponsored by a member to get in. Nobody can just walk in the door and sign up. Even if someone knows and sponsors you, the membership board has to officially approve all members by a vote. Not everyone gets in automatically.

"So perfect that Tori and Rich are going to be our sponsors. Love them, and they are our best friends," Ally says with secure pleasure.

"Rich is a bit dull on the course, but overall, it will work out," Todd says as he peeks back over his shoulder at the golf course.

Typically at any club, social climbers, social outcasts, social gossips, and social butterflies are everywhere. There are also the club flirts, the cheating husbands and wives, the divorced and remarried members, the younger and older couples, and members' kids and guests.

It is often a complex, interwoven, and affected scene, the events of which are recapped by determined parties at the other club on Sunday: church. If not at church, brunch on Sunday accomplishes the same thing.

There are the typical cliques and cliques within the cliques. There are the tennis players, the sailors, the golfers, the riders, the pool people, the ladies who lunch, the benefit committees, the partygoers, the members, and on and on. Of course, there are parties and benefits outside the clubs that still maintain the same social circles. All of this must be carefully navigated in this complicated country-club lifestyle, or you risk falling out of favor in the social scene for yourself, your family, your children, and your family legacy at the club, if there is one.

"I just want to officialy get in soon because being constantly 'on' socially and judged at events and dinners is so beneath us," Ally says with an annoyed look in her eyes. She stands, looking down at the boathouse and the dock past the parking area.

"Ally, it's all part of the process to get in. Just let it happen, and soon we will be all official. Can't see why we wouldn't be anyhow," Todd reassures her calmly.

"It is so connected to the church and benefits and volunteering at the thrift store for me that I can hardly escape—even at the nail salon." Ally has exhaustion in her voice.

"You enjoy that with your friends, and it is just part of the social canvas here in Shore Haven; you know that. Most women would not complain about that if they wanted to get into the club. There are just parts you have to deal with if you want it," Todd explains as they get back into their luxury car and drive off home.

"I just want to be in. Talk to your friends after church too on Sunday, and be sure to socialize there," she demands of Todd. "It's just an extension of Shore Haven Country Club."

It is true. One must belong to one of the churches in Shore Haven. Attendance is required every Sunday, except in the summertime when everyone is away at their houses in the Hamptons or on Nantucket Island. There is the same thread of social gossip from Shore Haven Country Club woven into the landscape on Sunday.

Everything needs to be carefully quantified, assessed, and determined almost from entry to Shore Haven if you were not born and raised here. Acting quickly to get your kids into the right club, the right day schools, the right country-club programs, and the right college ensures that they will have the same future on Wall Street and the same opportunities at the clubs when they want to become members eventually. It is about legacy at the club for your children too.

"Tori's boys are going to be at the same day school as ours this year," Ally mentions to Todd as they drive along the shore with decadent homes scattered across the hills.

"Everything is falling into place for us, Ally," Todd assures her, taking out his expensive sunglasses to shield his eyes from the glare of the sun off the water. It is just past Labor Day, before daylight saving, and the sun is still strong and low across the afternoon sky.

"Everything except the club is happening. I would do anything to get us in there," Ally says, thinking hard about how to ensure their membership.

"We'll get the letter one day soon, and Rich will tell us beforehand, I am sure," Todd reminds her. Rich is on the membership committee; he is their sponsor and best friend.

"After we get in, let's go on a trip to get out of this social drama for a bit. Let's escape together and reward ourselves. Maybe Grand Cayman?" Ally says, thinking about a luxurious beach vacation over the holidays.

In Shore Haven, escaping the scene during sponsorship time or any other is not possible. Members shop at the same boutiques and gourmet pantries. They are always spotted at the nail salons, the spas, or the day and prep schools. They host intimate dinner parties, attend church, dine at local spots, and attend local events. It is a complex weaving of club and non club life in Shore Haven. You always want to be in and never out among the social elite in Shore Haven.

"I know. We have to just go along with it all for now to get in," Todd reiterates neutrally. Getting in does not matter to him as much as it does to Ally. He just enjoys playing golf on the weekends, and it is a spectacular eighteen holes overlooking the water with the beach club and boathouse for sailing off in the distance.

The country-club scene in Shore Haven is representative of most such clubs across the country, both on the surface and structurally. Each has moral and social dilemmas. The Bennets will find that Shore Haven Country Club has a bit more to offer than that as they seek membership among this elite group.

CHAPTER 2

Getting In

*S*o Ally and Todd Bennet put their application in officially at Shore Haven Country Club, and their best friends Tori and Rich Hunter are their sponsors. It is the most prestigious club, even if you just sit by the pool with a gin and tonic and never actually play tennis, golf, or sail. This is perfect for the Bennets.

Tori Hunter is Ally's former college roommate from Princeton. The Bennets have been guests of Tori and Rich's at Shore Haven Country Club numerous times. Official membership will remove the Bennets from sponsorship stigma and elevate them as real members.

It is all woven into their social repertoire of clubs, benefits, golf games, and Sundays at church. Their children will all grow up at the club, go off to college, get married here, and eventually become legacy members. That is just how it works—or is supposed to work.

Today, Ally and Tori sit outside on the patio and eat lunch together at the club. It is a warm afternoon just past Labor Day. It is not officially fall, although everyone is back from summer vacations. The kids are over at the pool with the nannies.

Ally is the typical slender, statuesque blonde with long hair and blue eyes. She represents the quintessential country-club wife. Tori Hunter is equally attractive, but a bit shorter with dark features. The pair is as coiffed and refined as everyone else dining on the patio, if not more so.

Of course, they both use the latest beauty lines. They go to the best salons for highlights. They have the best dermatologist to maintain their appearances in their competitive social circles. Typically, they get mani-pedis together at the salon before dinner at the club on Saturdays, and that is the only time they are seen in their yoga pants.

Tori and Ally have never done yoga, actually, and it is not offered at the club. They confide in each other about their recreational dermatological treatments and compare results often as they compliment each other. This is also just part of the social landscape.

Ally asks Tori, "Who does your highlights at Trevi Salon? They look perfect."

"Kristy is doing them again. You know how I am. I rotate back and forth between her and Alexa and Kristy depending on what I want," states Tori.

"I need to do some around my face again. It is time to keep that summer blonde," Ally remarks, pointing to her hair and showing Tori where she needs the streaks. "When are you due for your next dermatological treatment?" Ally asks Tori with a knowing smile. "Because it looks great, and you look so well rested and no crow's-feet at all! I am impressed. Ally looks more closely at Tori's eye area.

They both often did recreational dermatological treatments of sorts that were never really mentioned to keep up appearances, just another layer of the club landscape.

"You know how it is. I never tell Rich about it. He just thinks I am naturally gorgeous. Which I am," Tori jokes, relishing in her inflated sense of self.

Rich is her husband, and he knows Tori is high maintenance, as most women in Shore Haven are. They have high expenditures at the salon and equally as pricey designer shopping bills. Ally and Tori have the most stylish clothes from the local boutique stores sharing the same personal shopper. They never shop discount or even mention it.

That is just part of the country club life too. Rich and Todd accept it because each likes an attractive wife, and image is important to maneuver your way up the country club social ladder.

Ladies wear the latest and donate last season to the thrift shop or consignment store where others snap up the barely worn designer bargains. That is where Tori and Ally work once a week to give back, or at least give the appearance that they are.

"Love your outfit and love the shoes," remarks Tori about Ally's outfit, admiring it head to toe.

"Oh, you know, our mutual personal shopper helped me again. What can I say?" Ally says with a smile.

Todd knows Ally loves to shop and shops too much. He actually has her on a budget, if you can call it that. It is well funded for their life, and any other woman would love to abscond with her fashion budget or any of her designer clothes. It is more like a clothing pension than a budget; it's funded well and grows over the years.

The ladies met freshman year at Princeton and stayed roommates after college in the city with their first jobs in advertising. They both married their first husbands and got their first houses in Shore Haven together. They also got their second houses on Nantucket.

Prior to that, like all young ingénues, they summered in the Hamptons in shares as singles. They would never actually summer there now; it was too noisy for them with the city buzz. Although, they loved the beaches and went when invited to the horse shows and parties by friends.

Ally sips her glass of white wine, heartily savoring it, and says to Tori, "Todd and I really feel Shore Haven Country Club is right for us and love that you and Rich are our sponsors. We can't wait to get our official notice in December when they are mailed out. But, Rich will tell us first, right?" Ally's voice is intense.

They usually meet and decide in November, and notices of membership acceptance come out around December. Because Rich is on the membership board, the Bennets are a just about in Ally surmises, and as best friends, of course, she's sure he will tell them first.

"You're sure to get in. SHCC is so right for you, and we love sponsoring you and Todd," Tori mentions and delights as she enjoys her salad of endive and bib lettuce with a touch of champagne vinaigrette.

She does not ever eat bread or butter. Tori and Ally are both very conscious of their bodies and weight, especially with all the competition at the club. She and Ally are in their late thirties and look amazing, but there is always that proverbial younger other woman around town or the latest divorced someone looking for someone else's husband.

"The kids love the pool. Can't get them out, especially on a day like this. Just as well. Gives us time to talk. Next spring they can start sailing in the junior program. The boys can learn golf too and start playing with Todd when they get older. Help them on Wall Street later. All the deals are made on the back nine anyhow," Ally quips smartly to Tori.

"Lily and Taylor will both be married here one day too, I am sure," Tori says, nodding her head between bites and acknowledging Ally's comment about the boys. Her mouth was full, so she could not reply except about the marriage part. Lily and Taylor are Ally and Tori's gorgeously appropriate teen daughters respectively.

Of course, the Hunters want the Bennets to be official members at SHCC. However, secretly, Tori wants to enhance her social status at the club further so that when she walks by people, they know who she is because her husband is or was club president. New membership means money for the club. Bringing in new members to the club is an unspoken plus whether you are on the membership board like Rich or not. The club always needs to be funded by the members. People have talked about all of this stuff for centuries at the clubs.

Not only is Rich on the membership board, but he hopes to be club president one day soon as well. There is an unspoken prestige to that position even when you are out of office. You are always regarded and mentioned as the past president and held in high regard nostalgically for your term.

If he can spearhead a new membership drive and bring in the most people, it will enhance his worth at the club furthering his chance of taking on the two-year term as club president. He is trying to get on the board as treasurer now too. The way it works is that you get on the board and eventually get a term as club president. That would mean more prestige at the club for the Hunters. Tori was about prestige more than Ally even realized, but Ally wanted that too and desperately wanted in at the club.

"It'll be so fun to be here officially, and then I can come and go whenever I want and invite whomever I want to the club like you can," Ally states with a smile as she sips her white wine, which is actually her favorite California sauvignon blanc.

It is almost so steamy on this late summer afternoon that she should have gotten a white wine spritzer on ice instead. Dressed in her navy skirt and white shirt, she thought she'd be cool enough, but it was a humid day on the patio for just past Labor Day.

"One day all of the kids will join and be legacy members at Shore Haven Country Club," Tori continues. She probably would have her daughter Lily's wedding there one day in the main dining room with the reception on the lawn in the tent if it was nice out. It was already planned out in her mind. Tori had on a navy sundress with her tortoise shell aviator sunglasses looking stylish and sophisticated while eating her delicate salad. Everything had been picked out by her personal shopper, except for the salad.

"So you are going to have to come to every club event, party, and dinner and meet and greet the other members so they get to know you and Todd," Tori states with a smile.

She has her gold bracelets tastefully appointing her slender arms, and they show her modest summer tan off with the gold. Tori has an understated elegance of summer style and urban sophistication and likes to show that off at the club, even if she is just going to the club for lunch.

Most times she doesn't even have an activity other than lunch. Neither does Ally. Lunch is activity enough after a morning of boutique shopping.

"Last winter was so long and dreary. It was so great to be on Nantucket all summer. Hope this winter is not as long, or I will have to go Cayman again after Palm Beach," Ally says.

Like most at Shore Haven Country Club, the Hunters and the Bennets travel to Palm Beach when the kids are out of school as a routine. They attend to benefits, the beach, the reciprocal clubs, and other events like nearby equestrian shows to keep busy and social.

Summers are always on Nantucket. Maybe in the Hamptons, but they were too littered with the urban mentality still and the city buzz. Martha's Vineyard was not really quite Nantucket, but passed for being away if you had to go there. Nantucket was preferred. and Ally's parents had always gone there with them as kids to their house in Dionis along the gentle shore past Steps Beach, and she was about to inherit that too.

Nobody ever really spent time at the club or at church in the summer anyhow. Only the working husbands who came up on the weekends would meet in the grill room at the club for burgers together just to eat before the weekend on Nantucket. There was a stigma to not being away when the fall came around for the whole family. Sleepaway camp was okay, Europe was better, and summer at the beach was ranked at the top.

"So glad the boys got into Shore Haven Day School this fall. You don't want them anywhere else," says Tori, smiling and pleased about it. Plus, Tori will get a referral discount at day school because she got them in and will probably use it for some extra shopping Rich won't know about or Botox treatments. She'll keep that a secret from Ally too.

"So good that Lily and Taylor are rooming at Hills Prep again this year. They are just like us!" says Ally as she has some more wine. She glances over at the pool quickly but knows the nannies have it well in hand with the boys.

She is not worried about Taylor, who is a teen, sunning herself again with Lily poolside. They just got back from Paris for the summer together and have a lot to review before they ship off next weekend back to prep school. Probably talking about boys anyhow and bikinis.

"Love the outfit you wore last weekend to church and brunch. You should wear that again to the next benefit maybe," Tori says. "Will be so good to get you on board with everything here. Maybe we should play some paddle this winter since we both played tennis at Princeton."

"Love to, and Todd loves getting out on the course with Rich early on Saturdays, so that might work," Ally acknowledges.

"Just to be here to be seen is enough. We don't need a sport unless we want one," Tori says. Her real name was Victoria, but she did not like Vicky or Victoria. Nobody knew her at the club as Victoria, and her parents nicknamed her when she was a little girl.

"Dinner next Saturday night? The four of us, of course? Mani-pedis first, you and ne?" Tori asks Ally as she finishes her salad and empties her wine glass.

"Perfect. Love club dinners with you and Rich, even though the food is generally off," Ally answers with enthusiasm and a witty smile. The food was never quite gourmet. It was acceptable to the palate for the purpose it served. Members always had something to say about it or the new chef.

Everything is setting up for the Bennets to get into the club without question in seems. Ally already imagines their name in the registry book that all members get so they can contact each other. Rich Hunter will push for them to be voted on affirmatively in the November meeting. The Bennets met all of the requirements. They are successful, affluent, and attractive; drive nice cars; know the right people; have a magnificent home; and have three attractive, intelligent children. Todd is also a very skilled golfer who should help the club win interclub and intra club championships too.

It is all so serendipitous so far in the process. The application is in to the Shore Haven Country Club. The Bennets are socializing, and there are no social snags so far. Ally thinks the process is working out well. It will only be another few months before the membership board meets again to analyze applications, review them, and send out the acceptance letters. Then, they will be in.

Most people get in if they fit in properly. If you are in favor generally in the social scene outside of the club, then you have a better chance certainly. Socialites fall in and out of favor quickly with unreturned phone calls, e-mails, texts, and invitations. It is important to stay with the in crowd and do all the right things so you are in favor.

Tori only told Ally stories of existing members' second and youthful wives not getting approved if they had too many gin and tonics around town and became obvious handfuls publically. The club did not want new members such as those.

In the past, there had been scandals at the club when older women married significantly younger men or older men married extremely younger women as second marriages. The club had to protect itself and screen the new spouses carefully for membership as well. This was not the case with Ally and Todd Bennet; there was no scandal thus far.

So, unless something catastrophic happened, Ally was sure that they were going to get in to the country club officially. Then she could come anytime she wanted and remove the inconvenience of being sponsored and being just a guest. They would be real members.

CHAPTER 3

Next Saturday Night at the club

*U*sually at the country clubs in the area, rumor has it that the food is never any good. At Shore Haven Country Club, the rumor is true. If you are not going through sponsorship, wanting to be seen, or using your minimum monthly dinner fees, members eat out at local restaurants or have exclusive private dinner parties. If you are not invited to a private party on a particular night, then you are out of favor. You want to be included in those select gatherings. Tonight, it's dinner at the club instead for the Hunters and the Bennets.

The main dining room at the club overlooks the water with a shaded outdoor terrace. Tonight it is still warm for a late summer, early fall night, so the Hunters and Bennets ask to be seated inside, even though gin and tonics are always a treat on the patio outside where one can watch the sailboats grace the sound before the winter chill arrives.

"I called ahead to reserve the table by the window, under Hunter," Rich says to the dining room host, Benjamin, who had been there for years and years. Benjamin is a middle-aged, refined, bright-eyed man with elegance and class. He is dressed in his club uniform, which is a crisp white shirt, black dinner jacket, and black pants.

He seems to be the only one who respects the privacy of the members. If he takes in the gossip at the tables in the hush of the dining room, he files it away and never opens it again. That is how he has remained at Shore Haven Country Club for his entire career. There is an art to discretion that some club members could learn from Benjamin.

"Right this way, Mr. and Mrs. Hunter," he says as he also acknowledges and welcomes Mr. and Mrs. Bennet. Benjamin then leads them off to the table by the window Rich Hunter had reserved.

The host of any typical country club sees lots of different couples and hears many stories over the years. Hosts must remain silent about these things although, they could probably write books. It is just part of club life, and Benjamin knows that well. He sees many new girlfriends come in with newly divorced gentlemen who vied for their attentions and vied for club life in general.

At Shore Haven Country Club the kitchen staff and chefs are upheaved every now and then when a new president or board takes office. Sometimes, the new president and board decides it can all be done better. Even then, they poach chefs from another local club or restaurant nearby, keeping with the standard country club fare that most members complain about over and over again. It's all the same wherever you go, both the food and the social climate at these clubs.

"Wonder what they will be out of tonight," says Rich with sarcasm. "I usually like the filet, but they always seem to be out of it on Saturday night." Rich smirks and looks at the menu for another selection.

Rich Hunter is a handsome, somewhat stocky, blond-haired and blue-eyed man. His passion on the weekends is golf and teeing off early on Saturdays unless there's an early snow. Todd is no different, and they play together often.

Rich had known Ally for a long time before she met Todd in the city and moved up to Shore Haven. The three used to house share in the Hamptons before they all got married. Rich never really knew Todd fully but accommodated him into their foursome at the dinner table and on the back nine. Now, he is sponsoring him at the club and hopes he'll help them get intraclub championships going again.

The dining room is a creamy neutral white with beams of wood and grand chandeliers with formal dinner services set out on the tables. Most of the old clubs had to renovate to attract new, younger members with the changing tastes in design and decor. Most clubs just went to typical blank canvases and removed the old charm to attract the younger professionals. It all seems like a sterile hotel at most in the area, and Shore Haven Country Club is no different. The members often complain about the renovations going over the budget. It's really something idle to talk about if there is nothing else to say at dinner.

"So, do you think that we need more color here in the dining room or more artwork after the renovations?" Tori asks Ally.

A lot of women at the club claim to be designers or decorators or realtors to maintain at title of some sort. In reality, most just don't work and like being at the club for lunch, but have to still carry a title or have a project or work on a benefit and be a part of a committee. Like the country club, you need a personal label as well.

Tori claims to have reinvented herself as a decorator and designer in her new life. Ally knows it's a falsehood, as Tori only designs her life and not a living room. However, Ally does not burst her bubble and allows her to believe that she is, in fact, a designer.

Women support each other and their efforts and nod their heads politely, acknowledging some type of career or something or other exists when they question whether it did or did not. The dreaded question at a this club or any country club dinner table for a woman is, "What do you do for a career?"

"It is a bit sterile and needs a splash of color or some stunning floral arrangements seasonally. Maybe a punch of color generally would work well," Ally states, looking around the room. "Not blue or denim blue or nautical-themed colors just because we are by the water. Maybe a fern green or something to bring the outside in."

Tori agrees and says, "Denim is never allowed at the club anyhow in any respect, and I certainly would not want it on pillows or chairs."

Denim is never allowed at this or any other country club on any occasion. Members or guests would immediately be sent home for wearing denim, and nobody did it. So, Saturday night dinner at the club is respectable in collared shirts or button-downs and a jacket, preferably a tie, for men.

The ladies, as always, are in something attractive, probably picked out by the local personal shopper at the boutique in town. Everyone works with the same personal shopper, who also knows local gossip from the dressing room.

Todd sets up as a tall, handsome, dark-haired, and dark-eyed man to the contrast of Ally's light features. The Bennets are an ideal physical couple with attractive and handsome features.

Women vie for Todd's attention even with Ally around and often vice versa, but Ally never responds to advances. Todd is not an outwardly flirtatious type or a typical player. For the most part, he has been loyal to Ally during their marriage so far.

After a round of gin and tonics with white wine for the ladies, Rich states, "Eight o'clock in the morning okay with you tomorrow, Todd, for tee off?"

Teeing off Saturday and Sunday at the club and playing a solid eighteen holes was just the thing Todd needed after a long week on Wall Street commuting back each night.

"Definitely. Eight o'clock works," Todd answers, glancing from his menu around the dining room.

Ally and Tori discuss the latest benefit at the boutique store in town called Hatherley's. It is typically some fashion show that benefits some cause. Usually, after lunch out, it is their go-to shop each week for new dresses, bags, and scarves. They shop with their common-denominator personal shopper, who promptly sends their husbands the bill at the end of each month.

As Todd looks around the dining room while Ally and Tori chat, he spots a very sophisticated blonde woman at the table in the corner who seems to make direct eye contact with him several times.

Her eyes are piercing, poignant, and sexy. She appears to be a bit younger than Ally and is wearing a black, fitted sundress that shows off her shoulders and remaining summer suntan. She is with another couple, and it seems obvious that she is there alone. Todd tries to look at her ring finger from afar, not that a ring matters to Todd.

Precocious, stunning Casey Tate is single by way of a recent divorce. Casey got the club and the house in Palm Beach. Her ex-husband kept the Hamptons and a few other things. Casey got Shore Haven Country Club because her parents were founding members and had an early number. There was no way her ex was getting that. They have no kids, so it was less complicated and a quick divorce. Rumor has it that she had cheated numerous times on her ex around the club.

"That's Casey Tate over there," Rich explains. "She took her husband to the cleaners when they got divorced, even though there are rumors that while he was on the back nine, she was somewhere else with someone else." Rich keeps his voice quiet and wears a devious smile. "You'll meet her soon. She's on the membership committee and is club president, believe it or not." Rich whispers to Todd as he coyly nods in Casey's direction, connecting eyes to say hello across the dining room.

Casey quickly smiles back and looks away to her dinner party guests.

"She's always got someone on the side," quips Tori. "The real story is that she was with a married man who is not a member here lately." Tori leans in and whispers a bit more to Ally as Todd and Rich continue discussing Casey Tate and the membership board.

"I know her from volunteering at the thrift shop too. She comes in there sometimes to drop off stuff," Ally says, putting it all together. "She has really nice things she donates."

Ally had not realized she was club president at Shore Haven Country Club. It was a good thing Ally was skilled in the art of being socially fake to anyone and everybody. That way, you didn't offend anyone. She had been that way to Casey at the thrift shop and on the benefit committee when they had cross connected a few times. Now, she would have to be even more so. You never know whom you could be offending, so you are better off not offending anyone and staying above board and off the social out list by a misstep.

Casey is the type who validates herself through her conquests of men, most of whom are married to keep it safe for her. She was enormously wealthy and did not need another divorce and just liked to play the field for now. Everyone knew about her money and her affairs but accepted it because of legacy and her current presidency.

Tori has to play the game with Casey too and socialize even though she feels Casey is unscrupulous as the sexy club flirt. She's a legacy and the president. Tori has to be careful for Rich's sake, so she makes their relationship work on the benefits and at the club. Ally will have to as well now more than ever.

"What do you think of Casey?" Tori quickly asks Ally as she leans in to hear her response.

Ally looks over at Casey and whispers to Tori, "Attractive, yes. Divorced, yes. Makes it either awfully hard or awfully easy around here. I am sure it is a playground for her."

She notices every now and then that between bites of whatever she is eating Casey looks over directly at Todd. Ally swiftly notes this to herself. She says to Tori, "Don't look over, but she keeps staring at Todd."

"Casey never stares at anyone. They stare at her," Tori points out somewhat engaged in this delicious aspect of dinner.

Other women had made plays for Todd before, but not so blatantly and not so connected in the social scene. Ally puts her hand on Todd's and stares back at Casey to mark her man and savor the moment at dinner.

What Ally does not realize is that Casey has already marked Todd as her next affair, and she gets what she wants no matter what. Ally doesn't feel threatened by Casey. Rather, Casey challenges her to remind herself how much she loves Todd and their life. It also made Ally question how much she can compromise to get what she wants too because she wants club membership.

Todd's eye often wandered to various women over the years. Ally noticed it more and more lately. Their marriage appears rock solid to friends and family on the outside. Inside, however, there are humbling cracks, and things are off a bit off at times.

To date, there hasn't been an earthquake to rock their marriage and splinter them apart, but there are fault lines evidently and some tremors, mostly over issues with the kids.

That night at the country club, Casey Tate finished dinner first and walked out with a few more solid, direct glances to Todd. Sometimes for dinner, she land at the local restaurant-bar with other gal pals or maybe her latest tryst publically as is often the case. Men want to be seen with her, and because she's gorgeous and club president. Plus, being out with her is always covered up as club business.

Todd thinks Casey is sexy and to the point. Ally and Tori notice and take note of Casey's obvious flirtations with Todd.

"God, that woman is a flirt. She has a reputation of taking what she wants on or off the golf course. She's club champion here too,"

Tori explains to Ally quietly at the table. "She thinks she is entitled to everything and everyone. Just watch her. If you cross her, forget about getting in here."

Volunteering at church, the thrift store, and on benefits, Casey and Ally had crossed paths a few times, but she had never really been on Ally's radar. Men weren't involved at the benefits or thrift store, so Ally had never seen her in action.

Tonight, she realizes that Casey has marked her next conquest, and Ally may not be able to cross her if they want to get into the club. Todd may be her next trophy off the course.

Ignoring it for now, she knows she's the one taking Todd home to bed tonight. She knows she's on top, she's on that board, and she's club champion at home in the bedroom. Ally a mental note to give Todd her best performance in bed to top off dessert at the club.

Dinner at the club is pretty mundane and standard fare in every way, unless Casey is around to target practice with whatever new man she has her eye on. Tonight it seems to be Todd. She also likes the conquest of a married man without the complications of having a real relationship, especially since she's newly divorced. She likes to play and was a master at that art too.

Todd just sips his gin and tonic, calculating in his mind how to connect with Casey secretly. She's elegant, single, and sophisticated and club president. There is something attractive about that power, that strength, that confidence.

Before ordering dinner, he and Rich talk about what club was best for each shot and about the intra and interclub tournaments coming up. Todd doesn't look back at Casey as she walks out, but h knows her name and suspects he will connect with her again at the clubhouse after golf. He'll make a point to be visible this weekend and next.

"Have you had the dover sole here lately?" asks Tori.

"Yes. It was so good for lunch last week. Remember, after I got that new Prada bag at from the boutique?" laughs Ally as she smiles to Todd directly, knowing he disapproves of her excess spending.

She typically treats herself right, especially if Todd is going to have a dalliance. That validates her purchases even more.

Whether it was alcohol, shopping, or prescription pills, someone in every marriage medicated to placate themselves during times of fault lines in their marriage. Actual weekly therapist visits, which were talked about, were almost always considered trendy rather than necessary.

Nobody stays too late at the club ever. During sponsorship time, new members have to put in face time at the club to meet and greet and be seen. If they want another cocktail after dinner, maybe they continue on at the local restaurant-bar. That is where everyone who has been at the club on any given night would run into each other and gossip more. Sometimes, Casey shows up at one of the two spots, sometimes not.

Casey Tate was pleased about dinner earlier in the night and spies her new conquest at the club. She knows Todd and Ally are not members yet, because they aren't. Makes no difference to Casey either way. Except that Ally won't be able to cross Casey if the Bennets want to get in as a whole.

Casey would find out details about Todd personally from one of her social plebes, Olivia Hendricks. She is not even a member of the club. Rather, Olivia and her husband, Will, are perpetual guests of everyone.

They are known as social users and seekers who don't reciprocate but enjoy many invitations. Mainly because Casey is currently sleeping with Olivia's husband, and people seem to keep inviting the Hendricks out and about just because of the cache of sleeping with Casey. Will is aware of that too. It is as if Will's affair with Casey suddenly gave the Hendricks the "in" spot at every dinner table and occasion.

At heart, blonde and slim, Olivia is a social climber and a social gossip. This paired up perfectly with Will, her very attractive and handsome husband. Olivia is skilled at the art of social compromise to get what she wants out of life as well. No one was ever certain if Olivia knew about Casey and Will's extracurricular activities.

Casey and Will have a climactic relationship in the bedroom, but that is it for Casey. It is just that and nothing more and never will be. He is not from old money anyhow, so it just would not work out.

Somehow, along the way, handsome and attractive Will fell in love with Casey. He was originally just sort of using her bedroom as a social jumping ground but fell in love with her.

In this cross connected, intertwined town of Shore Haven, everyone knows everyone who is anyone from church, the club, benefits, and volunteering. Tori had warned Ally already that cute and charming Olivia Hendricks is a bubbly social climber. She explained that the Hendrickses were house users of Nantucket homes and not to invite them unless you had to. That is just how the Hendrickses were, They were social climbers who acted like they were from old money. Will wanted Casey and her old money. That was Will's plan now that he had fallen in love with her, not just her money.

After dinner wraps up, Ally gets into bed with Todd in a sexy bra and panties and gives Todd the best sex they have had in ages. She is thrilled to be on top and rides him like the horses she used to ride at the field club growing up.

The extra glass of wine helps Ally loosen up and get back into the proverbial riding ring. Afterward, Ally falls back in the saddle. She's not going to let Casey ride if she has anything to do with it, although she realizes that she has to heed what Tori told her. She can't cross Casey if they want to get into the club. Ally falls asleep dissecting that morsel.

CHAPTER 4

Window Shopping in Town

Ally and Tori volunteer in the thrift shop in town every Monday afternoon. They are on a committee there too. It's very important to give back and give the appearance that you are doing so.

As they walk out from the thrift store to their cars, they stand in the sunshine and move along briefly as they do some window shopping on the tidy, manicured little street. It was nice to relax outside before heading to the train station to pick up their husbands after a shift at the thrift shop.

Looking down the street in the direction of the church, Tori says, "Can't wait to hear the sermon on Sunday." She wonders what the topic will be.

Sundays in Shore Haven, except during the summer of course, are spent at church in the morning. It is just the way things are. Most people from the club attend one in particular, the clapboard one up on the hill by the water.

"The minister seems like he always has something to say that resonates directly with me," Ally says with an air of self-elevation so high it's as if the minister writes his sermons for her personally.

"He is amazing, and that is why so many people go on Sunday," Tori notes with a soulful look of tranquility and calm on her face.

They walk along from shop window to shop window just browsing. These stores are not the boutiques they usually spend money and time in. These qualify as just little shops to browse like eye candy.

"Yes, but I don't like how his wife gossips so much and pretends to not know. I have heard her whisper," Ally says, reflecting on the time she heard the minister's wife talking about Olivia Hendricks at the barbecue last summer. "Remember when she was talking about Olivia Hendricks and her husband while Olivia was practically right there? I thought she heard everything for sure."

"I remember. I prefer to work at the thrift shop on Mondays when she is not there to gossip. You know, when she has one or two glasses of wine, it's sometimes a disaster. Don't tell her anything," Tori warns Ally.

"I don't ever. I just listen to it. Well, the thrift shop and the church are good for you too. They are just another part of the country club, and it is good for you to meet all the wives and socialize every which way. Even with Casey on and off the turf," Ally explains with a quick wit and a smile.

While working toward becoming an official member at the club, it's good for Ally to meet the other wives out in town. So, Ally and Tori work there on Monday afternoons together.

Casey Tate just donates selected pieces of her gently used designer wardrobe to the store and pops in occasionally. It's the right thing to do to be seen donating anyhow.

Ally originally met Casey through Tori while working on a benefit committee for the church event last year. It's coming around again, and meetings will be starting up soon.

The annual charity fashion benefit committee really doesn't do much other than allowing an overly large number of members to participate in some form of coordination. Mostly it serves as a night out to socialize and gossip. Not much ever really gets done, except by one or two people who spearhead the committee.

"I hope Casey doesn't come in next week to the store when we are working," Ally says.

"I know. I prefer not to socialize with divorced women, even if she is club president. There is something about them that I can't relate to," Tori mentions as she ponders the horrors of singlehood again.

Tori and Ally walk down one side of the street looking at the little shop windows unimpressed, but they really just want to be seen. They cross the street and head down the other side for the same reason.

Divorce holds a social stigma in Shore Haven, as it seems to anywhere. No one admits that, though, they just shy away. It's almost as if divorce is a disease that no one wants to catch.

Many feel the sting of divorce with fewer invitations to couples gatherings and parties. Some chose to stay in meaningless marriages just for the title of belonging to someone shallowly without that sting of divorce. Many divorced women stick together until they remarry and then move out of the divorce club once safe in a new marriage.

"I could never be divorced," Ally says.

"Me neither," Tori answers emphatically, gasping and covering her mouth at the ridiculous thought of Rich and she being divorced.

Tori simply can not contemplate it and does not want to catch the disease in her house. Ally feels the same way, so they are polite to Casey, but not too in-depth. They wont' ever go out with her one on one. Instead, more of a surface relationship exists. Now, Ally takes more of an interest with her as far as gossip goes because of the club membership and her interest in Todd.

After Casey's divorce was final last year, it was oddly enlightening to see how many of her friends' husbands texted Casey to make private overtures to her. It actually boosted her confidence and aroused her sexual awareness and needs more consciously. The number of invitations surprised her. She was just that type of enticing woman.

"You know, Casey has been sleeping with Will Hendricks for some time," Tori dishes to Ally as Ally turns to look at a designer bag in the shop window.

"Really? So, why does she need to check out Todd?" Ally questions Tori politely before turning her attention back to the window. "What do you think of that bag?"

"The bag is okay. You have better." Tori notes. "Casey gets bored is the rumor. She doesn't like complicated. Rumor has it that Will is getting complicated, and she knows he is after her money."

Casey has been sleeping with Will for a while because of their sexual electricity. He was sort of notorious for stepping out on Olivia around town to see how far he could climb when he was in someone else's bed.

The pinnacle bed was Casey Tate's, and Will had been invited in. The problem may be that he fell for more than her money.

The Hendrickses are members of church, and that counts somewhat socially but not as much as the club. On Sunday they have to sit right up front and right near the minister to be seen. That is how they are.

Will has to repent on Sunday for accepting Casey's relentless sexual overtures and meeting at the boathouse or her house for gratuitous nights. Somewhere along the way, he fell in love with her, not just her money and social status.

"The fun part on Sunday is that everyone is there no matter where they were the night before or who they were with," Tori quips, detailing the setup on Sunday at church.

"Everyone just falls into place," Ally states. She wonders how they will fall into place with Casey floating nearby on the radar now.

Everyone is at church on Sunday. The Bennets, the Hendrickses, the Hunters, and Casey Tate, just not during summer. It's said that the minister and his wife have something so amazingly profound in their Sunday sessions that draws people. That is not the case. What draws the people is being seen on Sunday after Saturday night out to catch up and be seen again.

"It is not really Bridgette and Drew that make me go every Sunday," confides Tori. "It is really the social hour and to see everyone again from the club, I have to admit."

Ally nods and smiles in agreement.

The earthy and cosmetically bland minister, Drew Mason, and his wife, Bridgette, are much more than just the minister and his wife.

They are the neighborhood therapists and confidants for anyone who has a social secret.

Will had confided in them both about his affair with Olivia over late-night glasses of wine at the parsonage. They just looked through Olivia on Sunday with blanks stares so as not to give away their knowledge about Will's affair even though Will and Olivia walk in together, sit together, and leave together.

It is important to connect with the minister and his wife socially outside of church. It does not really matter whether they can save you from your social sins. Drew and Bridgette have to maintain support and membership for the church.

Church is really was another type of country club on Sunday that needs to be funded equally by the gossip, the members, and the worship. So, Drew and Bridgette Mason play their cards properly among the social web.

The Masons are close personal friends who come to dinner at everyone's house and are invited to every event in town. Drew and Bridgette were seen at the club and all of the local events and places in town always. It added some sort of spiritual and social prestige having them there.

It's as if your event is more complete if Drew and Bridgette are there. The Masons are the ones you would go to if you had trouble in your marriage or anything going on. It was important to really be in their tight circle to be anybody at the church.

"I think Todd is more interested in going to church this Sunday to see who he sees there after the other night at the club," Ally offers knowingly.

"Casey will be there to be seen, and she walks in alone and sits alone," says Tori. "Can you imagine doing that?"

"Never," quips Ally as they walk down the street farther toward their cars.

"Well, this was fun. See you at church on Sunday, and we'll definitely talk before," Tori says as she arrives at her luxury jeep and opens the door to get in. They both kiss each other's cheeks in a quick European good-bye and head off to the train station to pick up their husbands.

Todd was never keen on the church part so much. Lately, he likes the social hour after church where he can talk to other husbands briefly about Wall Street and network his golf games. It is also another clear venue to view Casey Tate.

CHAPTER 5

Sunday Spots

When Ally and Todd walk into church on Sunday morning with their family, they sit in their regular pew. It's midway down on the right near the center aisle. It is their regular spot now, and no one else sits there, not even in the summer.

Olivia and Will Hendricks sit up front so that Bridgette and Drew can spot them. Nobody calls him Minister Drew; he is just known as Drew to everyone. Tori and Rich and their family belong midway on the left at the rear, so they can spot everyone and be seen by everyone coming in.

Often there is a slight hum when you walk in as people comment below their whispers about your lifestyle, what you are wearing, or who you are sitting with, or sleeping with, as the case may be.

"Look, there are the Bennets up front," whispers Tori to Rich. "Love her outfit."

"Well, there's Olivia and Will again," Rich whispers, questioning why they sit together when everyone knows about Will and Casey's intimate affairs at the club.

Casey walks in late every Sunday because she can. She confidently sits right on the aisle by herself, just in front of the Bennets. She never likes sitting too close to the Hendricks, even though she and Will have shared much more than Sunday service together over the years.

"Casey looks so good all the time," Tori mentions to Rich. Tori examines Casey's designer shoes and bag as she slowly swaggers by to take her seat on the aisle just moments before the service starts. That was her style every week, to walk in late, to be seen.

Will Hendricks is a fine partner between the sheets for Casey, but she is getting bored with his musings about leaving Olivia and getting married. Casey is sure she's not marrying Will. Todd will be her next conquest, and Will shall be a memory except at dinner parties and social events where they'll cross paths.

As Casey walks by to take her seat, Ally sees Todd obviously devouring every inch of her stealth, slim, and trim physique closely. Every man at church does.

Ally whispers to Todd, "Loved last night upstairs together," referring to their intimate dealings. Todd's eyes are clearly focused on Casey's tight and supple quarters as she struts in late in her stilettos with the red soles. Even he knows what brand they are because Ally has the same ones, and he paid the bill.

"Loved it too, sweetie," he whispers back in Ally's ear while his eyes are still focused on Casey's blonde hair tucked neatly into a low ponytail.

Todd wonders why Ally never wears her hair like that anymore when it is so sexy, even on a Sunday. He wonders what it would be like to undo Casey's ponytail and take off her dress. Somehow, he starts to hear the choir music, and his mind returns to his pew in church with Ally.

Will quickly looks back at Casey in her pew. Casey ignores him entirely as she glances at her song book. Casey knows she is totally done with Will as his advances are becoming socially obvious and ridiculous to bear. Their relationship had been in the bedroom and nothing more to Casey.

Casey could sit alone at church on Sunday and be confident and have anything she wanted. Divorce just strengthened Casey. It made her more determined to be the club golf champion. She also felt empowered and fulfilled by being able to select new members and new married men for future conquests.

This Sunday, in part of the sermon, Bridgette talks about fidelity and can't keep herself from staring like a laser beam at Will and then glancing to Casey.

"All relationships have compromise and redirections," Bridgette goes on to say in her wrap-up of the sermon. "People sometimes need different pieces of the puzzle to make it work." Bridgette is almost openly referring to and acknowledging Will's infidelity.

Many low whispers follow Bridgette's comment. Sometimes, she just does not think before she speaks surmise many worshipers, and they let her get away with being somewhat irresponsible with the gossip she is privy to.

All relationships need compromise. At least they do if they want to be members at the club.

Most men at church and the club know that they could never have this kind of woman. All the married men aspire to sleep with Casey and are always on their best behavior, wondering if they'll be next in line.

Todd cannot keep his eyes off her supple assets as she stands up and sits back down at various points in the service.

Ally whispers to Todd, "Let's go to brunch after and celebrate last night."

After church at coffee hour, Casey chooses to purposely ignore Ally. She just circles with Tori and Olivia for a bit before swiftly departing. She never likes to stay too long anywhere and always arrives late and leaves early. It's her style. You never know if you're in or out with her either, and you always want to be in with Casey Tate.

Todd and Ally head off to brunch at the local spot together, though Todd has only savory thoughts of Casey on his mind and not the numerous croissants. Brunch is delicious, but not as fulfilling as a moment with Casey.

Todd wonders if Casey will walk in and sit at the bar with her friends after church as well. He decides to keep an eye out for her while Ally and he dine at the table and sip mimosas.

CHAPTER 6

Benefits of the Thrift Store

$\mathcal{O}$n Mondays, Ally and Tory volunteer together at the thrift shop in Shore Haven. It is a time when they catch up together without the husbands and the kids if it is not busy and they can really talk.

Of course, they like to volunteer and give back, but it is also their time as friends to connect and gossip. It looks good on the outside that they are volunteering and serves as something to add to their social list for dinner conversation when they are asked the dreaded question about what one does for a living.

Most women give themselves the title of designer, realtor, professional organizer, or something similar to classify themselves even if they do nothing but lunch at the club. Truthfully, most are ex-professionals who left the city to raise their families with nannies and join the clubs in Shore Haven. They summer, they winter, and they fall appropriately into place.

Yes, some fall hard in love, like Will for Casey. Some fall in different ways along the way morally, like Ally trying to sort out if she should let Casey have Todd momentarily to assure they be accepted at Shore Haven Country Club.

"Can't wait to officially be a member," Ally says to Tori.

"You'll get in if you don't cross Casey Tate," Tori says with a smile.

"I know she wants Todd," Ally states nervously. "I just want to get into the club and not think about the rest."

"Casey always gets what she wants," Tori replies sternly.

They sit behind the counter in the thrift shop waiting for customers to come in and chat to pass the time before they have to head off to their meeting for the benefit at the boutique later that afternoon.

"I am resigned to that fact with Todd actually. Surprised?" Ally affirms to Tori. Ally's eyes light up about joining the club officially, knowing what she has to compromise to get in. "Remember what Bridgette said in her sermon? All relationships require some kind of compromise."

Tori suddenly looks pleased with Ally's revelations.

"Plus, Todd has cheated before, and I have ignored. I've never even mentioned it to you," Ally confides. "Nothing is that different now except that I want to be officially in."

"So, don't cross Casey," says Tori emphatically. She's pleased, knowing that if the membership process continues smoothly, it also helps Rich with his agenda too.

"It'll be a one-time thing, and I will just shop until I drop at the boutique and buy a lot of expensive things like I always do," Ally says with a smile, knowing that the affair is imminent either way. Knowing that she medicates with expensive toys and things when she suspects Todd to be unfaithful.

"It'll probably be a one-time thing if it happens because Casey gets bored fast," Tori affirms gently.

Suddenly, the door opens to the thrift store, breaking them out of their barely palatable conversation. In walks Olivia Hendricks. She is everywhere in town, usually keeping up with the buzz and vying for new invitations for the weekend.

If she does know about Will and Casey's fling, she never lets it out, even to Will; their social calendar is full even though she is half-empty inside.

"Hi, ladies," Olivia calls out as she walks in.

"Hi, Olivia," Ally responds. She signals for Olivia to come over to the counter to talk to them more intimately.

"Tell us what you know about Casey Tate," Tori says immediately, knowing that Olivia half knows about the affair with Will but pretends not to publically.

"Well, she is divorced and loaded and club champion, as you know. She also goes after and through a lot of men at the club," Olivia says with a concerned yet aloof look in her eyes.

Both Ally and Tori look down and away so they don't have to make eye contact that would disclose their knowledge of the affair. Olivia pretends to be oblivious to it for her own reasons.

"Casey is an operator, not a climber, but she likes conquests. She likes to know she gets what she wants, and nothing stands in her way," explains Olivia, who has a bird's-eye view of Casey's operations with Will.

"Seems she has an eye for my husband, Todd," Ally says, breathing a long, deep sigh.

"Well, Casey is trouble, and memberships are approved by her ultimately, so if you want to get in, you have to play her game," Olivia states knowingly from experience. That is why Will is allowed to go under the radar to Casey. Olivia likes the social benefits she receives from that relationship.

"We just want to get in to the club," Ally says, knowing that an unspoken bond has just been formed between her and Olivia. Both of their husbands are conquests of Casey's for various reasons.

"You will get in if you do what you need to do," Tori pointedly says to Ally.

"Wow, I don't know what I would do if she were after Will," Olivia answers coyly, pretending to be astonished.

"Don't give that a thought, Olivia. She's after Todd, and I can handle it," Ally states confidently.

Ally almost prefers that Casey take Todd over Will to ensure their membership at the club. The membership at the club means more to her than Todd's questionable fidelity or infidelity.

"The club matters to me now. I don't care about the rest," Ally says, adamantly and publically compromising to Olivia and Tori. Tori smiles, almost delighted inside, because Ally has chosen to ignore the affair. Rich is going to be pleased that their acceptance into the club will all be seamless with no issues.

Ally feels badly for Olivia's blind eyes but figures Olivia has her own agenda for choosing to ignore Will's blatant rendezvous with

Casey. People rationalize things for selfish reasons. She remembers what Bridgette said.

"All relationships have compromise. That's what Bridgette said last Sunday," Olivia reminds them with a soft smile.

That is what Ally surmises and decides to be just like Olivia and ignore the imminent affair for personal social gain. Everyone rationalizes or compromises something to get somewhere. Church even said it.

Ally and Olivia compromise their husbands. Tori compromises their friendship by looking the other way for Rich and the committee and the club and his future. There's a club trophy for everyone who wants it, but it comes often with some sort of social price tag.

Tori suggests, "Let's all go to the benefit meeting tonight together. We'll show Casey we are all on board for Ally's membership to go smoothly."

"Where there is a will, there is a way. No pun intended," Olivia quips with a smile.

As soon as it is four o'clock, Tori and Ally close up the thrift shop, as their shift has ended. Ally decides even if she does let Casey have Todd, it will only be for a short time until they are officially welcomed into the club as members in November. After that, All will take him back boldly.

Ally realizes everything in life is not free. Often you have to give something to get something. After all, the sermon in church had just said that is how relationships work.

Tori ponders why she's secretly hoping the affair with Todd and Casey happens. She doesn't ever want to be a bad friend to Ally and wants to stand up for her if Todd's going to be unfaithful again.

On the other hand, it would buy something for Tori and Rich. Todd's affair with Casey would placate her, and then she would approve them for sure. That would purchase status at the club for the Hunters now, and it would purchase potential for the future for Rich to be the club president.

Maybe if Ally and Tori go to Paris for a few weeks later in the fall it will allow that infidelity to occur more naturally and get Ally away from it. They can shop their way through Paris. Tori decides to suggest the trip, although she realizes that with prep and day schools in session and activities and benefits getting into full swing, it will be hard to step away.

Secretly, Olivia would also benefit from Todd and Casey having a fling. If Casey moves on to Todd, Will may be home and available more to Olivia and their social calendar. Casey will be happier knowing that Will won't keep posing the thought of leaving Olivia anymore, and Casey will keep the invitations coming their way to keep him out of her hair. It's a win-win for Olivia.

Olivia likes going to the polo matches, the horse shows, the sailing cup races, the benefits, and the art shows. She's already an artist in the art of compromise. She knows how the give-and-take works in the social scene whether or not she admits it to Ally and Tori. In Olivia's mind, Ally is a novice at the art of living in the club world.

Olivia decides to have Drew or Bridgette mention to Will that Casey's affections have turned to Todd. Everyone has to protect their own interest at the club whether they're members or just over invited guests.

CHAPTER 7

The Benefit Committee Meets

*E*very Monday at five o'clock in the church conference room, the Church Benefit Committee meets in season. Usually, the ladies all bring something to snack on, and they often start with some wine to relax together and catch up. It is not all about the event and the meeting and agenda; it is about socializing, gossip, and catching up with whoever is there and on whoever is not.

It is important to be on some committee, have some importance, and contribute to something. It is noted among the members of the church and the SHCC if one is not. Serving on a committee is another way to give back, socialize, and hear the latest gossip.

Casey Tate sits on the sofa with Olivia, Tori, and Ally. They seem perfectly cozy in the church library, as if nothing is wrong. The three have agreed to pretend to Casey that everything is okay even though it is known Casey has marked Todd next in line after Will.

Because it is a church meeting on church grounds, Bridgette is of course there. She often goes out with the ladies for cocktails and dinner to socialize and piece together all the gossip and issues they tell her instead of telling their therapists.

Bridgette knows the meeting is not really all about the benefit. Of course, the benefit raises money for her cause. However, she knows that the socialites from the club will only come if other socialites on the committee invite them like Ally and Tory. She is caught up in the world of compromise and deceit too for her own agenda at the church.

People ponder whether to trust Bridgette socially. People have discovered that sometimes when she has a couple of glasses of wine, things become less confidential to Bridgette.

Casey has control of the final stamp of approval at the club. Ally knows she has to let Todd be the trophy for Casey now. She has heard from others like Bridgette that Casey has shut down other members for the slightest thing, even if the rest of the board agrees to approve the membership.

"How's membership going?" Bridgette asks Ally as they stand at the table with the wine and fill their glasses out of Casey's earshot.

"In the process and going forward rather well now," Ally says slightly rolling her eyes and staring back at Casey. "I know you know about Will, but now she wants Todd."

"Casey has ripped up other approved new-member applications in the process if she does not like just one little thing about someone," Bridgette tells Ally quietly in the corner. "Every relationship has a compromise or two."

"Yes, I know what you said in your sermon Sunday," Ally reminds her.

"Tell Casey when I leave that there is a green light on this project. She'll know what you mean." Ally resigns to officially give Casey her husband to assure her club membership happens swiftly and without question.

"Probably better than the red light. Just think of the boats in the harbor with port and starboard. Try to think of the port light that is green at the boathouse when you stare out at the boats on the sound at night," Bridgette says with a comforting touch to Ally's shoulder.

"Yes, going into Casey's port is more like it," Ally quips, knowing that it is understood now. "Just for membership time."

"How about you write her a note saying something to the effect of the green port light and not the starboard red light. She will understand your intentions of letting Todd be hers for membership time," Bridgette suggests.

"I really want us to get in, and now she is going to get in the way unless I compromise my husband to her at the boathouse," Ally reaffirms to herself. "The letter sounds plausible. She has to know I am open to this. I am tired of being so on all the time for everything and being so analyzed during membership time. I just want it to be done and be in and belong."

After giving it some thought, Ally agrees to write a letter to give to Bridgette to pass to Casey Tate. The rigorous social demands of getting into the club have worn on Ally as she has sought to affirm her status permanently by it being made official.

"Why don't you come over and talk to Drew and I one night, and we'll sort it out over some more wine. Every relationship has compromises, and not just one. There are many relationships compromised here in

Shore Haven, and you know about Olivia and Will and Casey already anyhow," Bridgette reminds her.

"This is more than a little compromise for me. Passing my husband over to the club president until we are official because she wants him? How can you say that from the point of view of the church?" Ally asks emphatically. It's clear she has some apparent surface moral concern.

"I don't say it from the church. I say it as your friend if you want to get in," Bridgette replies.

Ally pauses and sighs, knowing Bridgette is right. Ally does not want to be one of those members who tries to get in and has to retry and hope someone votes them in eventually.

That was a stigma worse than divorce, if you did not get in the first time and had to retry sponsorship. How many times it actually took you to get in was always remembered and talked about. People remembered, and it was socially costly.

Bridgette and Ally walk back and sit down on the couch with Olivia and Casey where they wait for the rest of the committee to arrive. The ladies sit and gossip about the latest new purse at the boutique and how five people already have it around town. They sit sipping their white wine together, aware and unaware of the sexual compromises between their band of husbands.

"So, since everyone else seems late tonight, let's get down to business and the agenda at hand. I have other agendas to get to later, so let's move on with the benefit," Casey suggests as she coyly looks at Ally.

Ally knows it is a reference to Todd. The green light had already been turned on in Casey's mind, and there was no sense of caution. Ally would not look to starboard red lights again. This course is set with port lights on now.

The Bennets need to get into Shore Haven Country Club, and it seems Casey Tate is the safe harbor both she and Todd require.

CHAPTER 8

Todd's Point

*O*f course, Todd Bennet is interested in Casey Tate whether or not the membership is in play. To his knowledge, membership is not affected by making the choice to sleep with Casey. There is no agenda on his part other than bedding a sexy, single club sophisticate who happens to be the club president.

Ally is more aware of the game being played by Casey regarding the membership. Bridgette slips Casey the note from Ally while making some references to port and starboard green and red lights. This all symbolizes Ally's conscious go-ahead for the affair with the agreement that safe harbor will happen for the Bennets when the membership committee makes a decision.

They had certainly connected that night at dinner, and he had watched her play on the golf course on the weekends a few times with Rich. Todd and Ally hardly ever sail, but they enjoy watching from the patio and the dining room. The boathouse is Casey's spot, and most members know that and stay away unless they are invited like Will often is.

Rich knows Todd is Casey's next tournament trophy at the club and Rich thinks it is flattering for Todd overall and approves. Rich knows that his chances of sealing the club presidency in a few years will be almost locked with a solid membership-drive track record.

"Saw Casey out there again today, and she looked like she was having a good game," Rich says to Todd on the patio at the club.

"She always looks good," Todd replies as he sips his beer with a cool arrogance about him.

So, this Saturday at the club it is still nice weather for golf, and Todd and Rich have just finished up. They are settling in to a nice, cold draft beer out on the patio and a burger with fries (the best thing on the menu), and they were never out of it.

To Rich, it seems like a win-win situation on and off the course for he and Tori. They can look the other way at the club for now and never talk about it.

Everyone has done that with Olivia and Will Hendricks for years. That is a talent he and Tori developed years ago at SHCC. They learned to be socially vapid and vacuous when necessary.

At SHCC everything is swept under the rug or forgotten over a few sips of white wine or gin and tonics. If you don't want to be gossiped about, it is better if you are present to avoid the opportunity to arise.

Casey already knows Todd's tee time from the clubhouse. She knows when he is about to finish up. She makes herself available in her golf skirt and cute sleeveless shirt on the patio at the right time.

Anything she wears from cocktail attire to golf sportswear makes her look exquisite. Other women say it's because she hadn't had children yet.

Casey decides to take off her golf glove, sporting her designer watch, and sit down with Todd and Rich. After all, she's the president and does have to meet the new members. She likes to show she has no wedding ring on her left hand, which is the hand she took the golf glove off; she's a righty.

"So, how were the greens for you today?" Casey asks as she orders a white wine and a shrimp cocktail from the menu. She knows it is all going on Rich's bill today. She never treats anyone at the club. Rather, they treat her if they want her company.

Todd takes the opening to publically say, "We should get out there sometime and play together, Casey."

"Well, luck would have it that there is a mixed tournament coming up at the club. You two should play in it," Rich says, looking at Todd and giving him the go-ahead to mingle with Casey without him next weekend.

Rich never wants to cross Casey with all of her social connections at the club and feels he elevated his position with her just now by connecting she and Todd publically.

"Yes, let's, we should practice beforehand, of course," Casey says before sipping her white wine with a delicious smile.

"Sometimes, I like to tee off into the water off the docks down at the boathouse just for fun when the club is closed and it is a nice night out," says Casey, playfully giving Todd a very warm and forward glance. She could really place her shots both on and off the golf course.

Todd notices Casey's perfectly toned and tan legs as she sits at the table in her perfectly fitted, white golf skirt. She has a warm smile with sun-kissed golden skin and blonde summer streaks and highlights that gracefully skim her face in the late afternoon sun. Whether they're real or from the salon, no one can ever be sure.

"How's your burger, Rich?" Todd asks, glancing over to see if any fries are left on the side.

"Well, it is not quite the tastiest thing on the menu," Rich answers with a knowing smile. He's fairly certain that Casey is probably a more delicious delicacy than the burger or anything else on the menu.

Casey looks across the patio toward the sailing center and boat docks. You can see it all from the outdoor patio. Parents usually sit here to watch their kids take lessons and have a glass of wine if the weather is nice enough like today.

Casey likes being near the boathouse on the dock at sunset if the weather is good and if the club is closed. Lately, it has been with Will, but she is getting tired of him and his pressure to be more than just a fling. Sex and conquests are Casey's style post divorce. She's still rebounding.

Having practically grown up at the club, Casey feels entitled to be anywhere she wants at any time at the club. Rumors are that she and Will often have sex in the boathouse after sailing classes are done and the boat boys go home.

No one has ever caught them because Will is clever enough to shield Casey's reputation further. He pays the dock boys money to give him the key, and then he closes up after he and Casey are through with their extracurricular activities. The boat boys never say anything and probably use the extra tips to buy new Top-Siders or extra gin for their tonics anyhow.

Todd has been unfaithful to Ally over the years both online and offline. Often, he's had one or two city trysts, but they never amounted to anything more. He's shielded by the suburbs and separates the city life.

Todd thinks Casey will be about the same. He's not concerned about messing up membership like Ally is. He just wants to sleep with Casey and connect, but he realizes he'll have to be cautious with Ally around the club too. He figures he will make it work because having Casey is worth any trouble he has to go through at home or the club.

City affairs have a separation between the city and the suburbs. When Todd catches the evening train home, whatever has happened in the city after a late lunch is left in the city. Casey, however, is at the club right under Ally's nose. Though Ally has been making herself scarce lately for reasons he can't sort out, he'll still have to be careful not to compromise his marriage. Divorce is a social stigma for men too, although not as marring as it may seem for a woman.

Todd thinks about how much he would love to touch Casey's body as he looks at her suntanned, perfectly toned thighs against her crisp white golf skirt again. She looks stunning sipping her white wine. She's confident. Todd wonders how a divorced woman can be so beautiful, confident, and sexy, and that draws him to her.

She has that something special. It's almost like she dresses as if every day is a first date. Married women tend to lose that flair of the first date once they get married and have kids. The single or divorced woman always has that unknown allure to Todd and to many men.

The reverse holds true for Casey. She finds married men alluring, and there are no strings attached for her. She keeps it discreet, but also knows who she plans to target next.

Todd continues to plan his move and hopes they too can sneak off to the boathouse later even if Ally is at the club having lunch. Rich probably will back up Todd that Casey and he are going to practice their golf game for member-guest and interclub mixed tournaments or something like that.

"Let's take our drinks down to the boathouse later, Todd," Casey negotiates knowingly. "We can tee off over the boats later too. It's fun! Meet me there at six for a round." With that, Casey stands up and puts her drink down on the glass patio table.

Todd nods in agreement as Casey turns and walks away toward the clubhouse. "Sounds like a plan," he states with a quick smile before resuming his beer sipping.

Rich and Todd both admire Casey's attributes and her sexy, sophisticated club style as she walks off.

"Meet her at the boathouse later? You're in!" says Rich with an enthusiastic stamp of approval. It's almost like Rich had just won the lottery. He realizes he has to tone it down to not show Todd too much enthusiasm because Todd doesn't realize Rich has ulterior motives for this relationship too.

"Thinking about it," Todd answers. The truth is he already knows he will go as he sips his gin and tonic heartily. The time has come to step up the game at the club, and there's no one else he's playing with in the city or online these days.

Will Hendricks is out of the picture now too, which Todd had heard from sources like Drew Mason at church. Rich had also mentioned that to him. Not that he cared, but it was a feather in his golf pants pocket that the boathouse door was open again.

"Ally's been so focused on the membership lately. It is all she talks about at home, and I need a break sometimes," Todd tells Rich, who looks even more pleased.

With Ally pushing at home about the club and getting in, spending time with all her benefit work, and talking about the way life should be for them, it's like she's pushing him into Casey's arms a bit anyhow. She's almost telling him to green-light the project with Casey.

Todd looks at his watch and sees it is nearly time to head to the boathouse and find Casey. He gets up, shakes Rich's hand, and thanks him for the late snack on the patio.

Wednesday night club sailing is the only time Todd and Casey will have have to worry about meeting at the club after work. Otherwise, the docks will be quiet, as the day sailors will already be tucked into safe harbor for the night. Plus, with winter coming, it will just be the frost bite sailors out there anyhow.

As Rich and Todd finish up their late lunch, the sun is starting to set as the page turns to early fall. What a perfect afternoon of golf, relaxation, and establishing a new game with Casey Tate on and off the course it seems.

CHAPTER 9

The Boathouse Affair

*D*own at the boathouse, Casey sits on the dock in the white Adirondack chairs making it obvious to anyone still at the club that she is still there. Her driver club and a few white golf balls are scattered near her feet, which are dangling elegantly with her perfect hot-pink pedicure. Her golf shoes are off, and she's not going to tee off anymore.

She begins to get a bit chilly on her skin as she holds the icy gin and tonic with lime for Todd. She already knows his drink of choice. Her white wine glass stands empty on the dock with the half-full bottle nearby.

Looking out down the greens toward the water, Todd spots Casey sitting on the deck in her chair and looking out. The boathouse is nearby. Rich had mentioned the rumors that the boathouse was one of Casey's obvious places at the club after dark, but he did not mention with whom.

Todd wondered but did not care either way. Tonight, it is his night with Casey, and he will enjoy all the benefits of her sexy summer tan and more.

Casey hears Todd come onto the dock and turns. "Glad you came by. Here's your drink," she says. "I am getting cold. Let's skip teeing off the dock tonight and take our drinks inside the boathouse and warm up. I have goose bumps." She stands up, takes her golf sweater, and gently drapes it over her shoulders, which are bare in the light from her sleeveless golf jersey.

Todd can't take his eyes off her shoulders and the way the late sunset light hits them. Her white skirt and navy sweater are just the perfect complement to her navy golf shirt, which shows her taught athletic shape off sublimely.

He reaches to get her wine glass off the dock for her and glances up back toward the clubhouse to see if he has been spotted by anyone. There are only a few cars left up on the hill in the lot, and Ally's white Range Rover is probably tucked neatly in the garage at home by now. He imagines Ally is waiting for him to come home before they head back out for dinner at the club later. Tonight, they are eating at the club at eight o'clock with the Hendrickses and the Hunters. Todd had some time, but not much.

"Let's go inside and play," Casey says with a seductive, sophisticated voice. She turns to stare into Todd's eyes with a coy and playful look.

Casey unlocks the door to the boathouse and steps inside where there are a lot of sails and nautical buoys. It smells a bit like the sea. There is a small light that Casey leaves on as she sexily sits on the edge of one of the boats that was turned over inside. Todd moves over near her, and without speaking anymore words, he pushes her hair back off her face, lifts her sunglasses out of her hair, and begins kissing her passionately.

Casey finds Todd to be equally sexy and decides to take him on fully in the boathouse that night as she holds onto the edge of the boat inside. Todd and Casey break all the rules in the boathouse.

Casey is a tremendous lover, and so is Todd, and their lovemaking exceeds anything he'd ever experienced before. It was a pinnacle nautical moment in the boathouse that night and Todd wants more.

Casey feels that extra vibe in their lovemaking, which is unusual to other trysts and exceeds Will. This was the start of her fling with Todd, and Will is to be cast out.

"So, how do you think your membership is going now?" Casey questions coyly, buttoning her golf shirt while adjusting her skirt with the other hand.

"Did I just seal the deal?" Todd asks playfully, putting back on his polo shirt and adjusting the very preppy golf belt that Ally had just given him for his birthday.

"Probably," Casey surmises, not yet sure exactly what deal they may have actually sealed besides the membership.

Todd walks with her off the boathouse dock into the sunset toward the parking lot. No one is there on the grounds, or so he thinks. Most members are home getting ready for another dinner out at the club.

Except for Will, that is, who sits in his Porsche watching from the hillside.

CHAPTER 10

What a Girl Wants

Ally questions where Todd is after his golf game, but does not question it. She is ready to go back to the club for another dinner and has on a sexy navy dress with a pink wrap over it.

"You're home a bit late," Ally states to Todd as he walks in the kitchen.

He's wearing his golf clothes and seems a bit flustered. "Ran late talking. Just need a quick shower, and we'll go back to the club," Todd replies, hardly looking Ally in the eye.

Ally had also heard from Bridgette and Tori that Casey mixes it up with Will at the boathouse sometimes and wonders if Todd had just made his maiden voyage.

Ally decides to pull herself together quickly with a glass of wine to relax along with some prescription from her doctor. She sort of savors the fact that membership may have just moved along quicker that evening.

Though the compromise of it all rattles her moral consciousness a bit inside and makes her edgy and nervous.

The Bennets have to continue to mix and mingle with other members and nonmembers to ensure their imminent membership decision is positive. Ally is on track and target with that and has dinner set up again. She has been seeing her psychiatrist more regularly during all of this to cope, but it is a medicinal coping that has been prescribed.

"Just going to unwind with some wine and wait for you, Todd," Ally says softly. She sits down with her wine and begins flipping through travel magazines. She slowly feels the medication relax her soul, which is riveted by dilemma and knowledge of Todd's contribution to attaining membership.

Todd can't get Casey off his mind as he runs up to the master bath to take a quick hot shower. She was breathtaking in the softly lit boathouse as she leaned on the upside-down boat that was stored inside with the nautical smell of the sea air. He can't get her suntanned legs off his mind. She's so ample, so taught, and so well appointed. Her confidence is alluring.

Will was foolish to fall out of favor with her by whatever he was doing. Todd had heard from Rich that Will wanted to leave Olivia for her, and that is what set Casey off. She likes it less complicated, and Todd is willing to keep it that way, for himself and for Ally and the kids.

Most divorced women just want to get married again to remove the social stigma quickly by getting out of that club and back into the married one. Casey constantly uses that to her advantage to harpoon new conquests at the club on the links and off simply because she knows she can. It's part of her validation, as her parents had basically abandoned her socially and skipped to Palm Beach permanently after her divorce.

Shore Haven was a social bubble on the weekdays with the kids for Ally. The men, like Todd, rejoin the social circle on the weekends when wives make the plans. Ally had already ironed out their social plans with Tori for the club this Saturday night again in a robotic fashion because she knows membership decisions are coming soon.

Todd joins in socially as the perfect doting husband trying to get the family approved into the club. He had just added the cherry on the membership cake with Casey, although he doesn't really know it. He also just unknowingly escalated Rich's chances of being club president.

Todd likes this new social scene that was set up for him. He gets to see Casey at the club, at church, and off the course for other activities. He feels hat the world of the suburbs has suddenly and succinctly connected as he punctuates his life with Casey's sexy attributes and his new affair.

He knows that downstairs, Ally waits patiently to head off to the club for Saturday night dinner to secure her spot socially at the club. After he gets his tweed jacket and tie on to dress for dinner, he goes to find Ally to help him put on his cuff links. The French cuffs are always an issue, but he always looks so sophisticated.

Ally whispers to Todd, "You look so handsome."

Todd kisses Ally on the forehead as she picks up her evening bag and wraps her scarf around her warmly. She's cold from their unspoken arrangement.

"Love you too," Todd replies, taking a sip of a wine Ally poured for him.

"I just want us to get into the club, no matter what, and not have to socialize like this to be approved anymore. It is so draining feeling like we are puppets on display at the circus sometimes. The not knowing and the pressure is annoying, and I don't want to have to do a round two of membership. That is social destruction here," quips Ally.

"Don't worry. We'll get in the first time and be member soon enough," Todd assures her, not knowing he just sealed everything at the boathouse and will continue to do so.

It all seems so socially convoluted yet socially acceptable to Ally, like a social puzzle being put together. Ally affirms that their marriage is solid for social purposes and realizes there are a lot of other women in her shoes making compromises to move ahead. Bridgette had reminded her and so did Tori and Olivia. Ally saw the ones Olivia made with Will, and now she was doing the same thing.

Ally has all she wants in life and just needs the club to seal her social status in Shore Haven with her friends like Tori. She is not going to rock the boat or the boathouse now. She decides to stay onshore by the pool and on the tennis courts and leave the offshore activities to Todd. The medications, therapy sessions, excessive shopping, and wine help her through it too. It's all part of the process her friends said, especially Bridgette.

The Bennets are ready for another Saturday night dinner at the club with their sponsors and friends. They set sail and head off slightly off course, but nevertheless finding safe harbor together for now.

CHAPTER 11

Club Dinner Party at Eight

*T*onight's club dinner table includes a cross connection of social climbers, social seekers, social sleepers, and social players. The Hunters, Bennets, and Hendrickses dine at eight o'clock at the club in the main dining room at the same table with the same sumptuous secrets on the menu.

Will slept with Casey, who now favors Todd. Olivia knows about both Will and Todd but never admits the part about Will. She only secretly gossips about Todd. Ally knows about both men and Casey. Rich and Tori know everything about all parties at the table and more.

Ally looks sophisticated and elegant in her navy dress and pink wrap, almost effervescing a glow of anticipation about being a real member. She ignores what may have happened that afternoon and why Todd was late. She rationalizes that it was for the greater good of the club. Todd can't figure out why Ally looks so radiant. It's as if she is on a first date with him tonight.

As she looks around, she notices Casey Tate is not in the dining room yet.

"Tori and I played some tennis this afternoon, and we won," Ally says to Todd and Rich with a smile.

"Oh, good ladies. We did pretty well out there on the greens. Todd is going to play in the mixed-doubles tournament soon," Rich says, patting Todd on the back obviously.

"You didn't tell me that," Ally says, looking at Todd almost happily. She wants into SHCC either way. "That should be fun for you and Casey!"

"How did you know I was playing with Casey?" Todd nervously asks, looking at Rich for help.

Will looks seriously disturbed by this news, especially after he had just witnessed them departing from the boathouse. In fact, he seems to be the one who looks a bit nervous about Casey and Todd playing in the club's mixed-doubles tournament. He had been invited by Casey last year and the year before to play. He seems flustered upon finding out Todd has replaced him.

"I played with Casey the past few years as her guest," Will states. He looks at Todd while avoiding Olivia.

"Well, there's always next year, pal," Todd replies sarcastically. "This is good for me to play since we are in the sponsorship phase of membership here anyhow. Right, Ally?" His question is a way to seek her approval publically.

"Absolutely, Todd. Go for it, and get a hole in one," Ally quips. She takes a long sip of her white wine as Olivia nearly gasps at her blatant answer and open acceptance of the apparent affair.

Olivia looks at Tori and Ally with a pensive smile. She is concerned that with Will out of the picture for Casey, their invitations may subside. However, what she doesn't realize is that Casey has her covered. She will keep the invitations flowing to keep Will happy socially, despite the fact that she's changed skippers at her helm. Olivia is not to worry.

"To the tournament!" Ally raises her glass to make a toast and extend her approval of Todd and Casey playing together. She also implies to everyone that she is open to the off-the-course activities to ensure they become full-fledged members. Ally had not been having too many trysts with Todd lately anyhow.

Just the last one, which would be their metaphorical and literal kiss good-bye for a while. Will seems to be the only one bothered by it all, it is becoming obvious to Olivia based on his change in demeanor and rudeness to Todd.

Suddenly, late and fashionable as usual, Casey walks into the club dining room looking radiant, sexy, and sophisticated in a black dress with heels. She heads over toward a table with Bridgette and Drew Mason from church who have been waiting for her arrival while enjoying cocktails in the grill room. The Masons suddenly appear and are led to the table with Casey in the corner.

Tori whispers to Ally. "Casey will probably tell them what is going on. You know, who's going to get in and who's not, among other things."

"We'll find out at the next meeting," Ally replies nonchalantly while sipping her wine.

Casey looks over and sees Todd and Will at the table together. She ignores Will's piercing eyes and looks directly at Todd as she walks by, still enhanced and invigorated by their early-evening activities dockside.

Will gets up and steps away from the table. He heads off to the men's lounge and tries to text Casey to meet him outside to talk later. Cell phones are never permitted in the clubhouse or on the grounds, and you can be sent home if you use them openly. Will is aware of that policy and does not intend for Casey to receive his text immediately; rather, he figures she will see it when she leaves. He asks her to meet him at the boathouse after dinner after he drops Olivia off at home.

Rich sits sipping his gin and tonic with an inner realization that his club presidency is imminent for the future. Things are falling in to place around him. He studies the menu to order for dinner and imagines the future as he walks into SHCC with Tori as club president.

The only thing of concern in the dining room tonight, other than what is on the menu and what the club is out of, is that Casey is dining with Bridgette and Drew. She'll probably tell them she slept with Todd and that Will is out. They might tell Casey that Will was going to leave Olivia sooner than she thought.

Will walks back to the table and watches as Casey confidently orders her wine and studies the menu. She never offers too much information to anyone; it was the other way around. Tonight might be different, though. Will has to talk to Bridgette and Drew later too.

He wants to leave Olivia and get into the real social-status scene with Casey now more than ever because he loves her. That has been his plan from the get-go, and falling in love helped his cause.

Casey plans to drop Will now for sure. Whatever happens to Olivia and Will is not her concern. Whatever happens to anyone is not her concern.

Will needs to stop the affair, so he can have Casey again. He cannot lose his social status in Shore Haven with or without Olivia. Olivia is his wife and social partner, but he has never loved her the way he loves Casey. He decides that he will just have to stop Todd. Now that he had seen them at the boathouse, he could get pictures the next time. Casey is so predictable.

In the social chess game of the social seekers at Shore Haven Country Club, it is just Will and Olivia who stand in Ally's way if Will forces Todd out. Ally vows at the table after one more glass of wine not to let that happen. She and Tori will have to have a secret lunch with Bridgette and find out what Casey said about Todd and Will.

"What's the matter, Will? Have a bad day on the back nine?" Ally inquires with a wit that alerts Will she knows what Todd is up to and accepts it.

"No, it was down at the boathouse where it all went wrong today, I think," states Will with a stern stare and solid warning to Todd, who ignores it.

Todd just sits tall and stares at Rich with a smile. Rich is pleased with Todd's steadfast resilience to Will's warnings.

Todd looks at Casey at the corner table and wonders when they will connect again, thinking back to the boathouse tryst.

Between hearty sips of gin and tonic, Will continues to think about his scheme and the pictures he plans to take of Todd and Casey at the boathouse. He must devise a plan to stop this affair.

CHAPTER 12

The Scandal at the club

With texts unreturned from Casey, Will starts to become desperate in his love for her and his jealousy of Todd. It is not fair to him that he has to sit idly and wait for Casey. It is not fair Casey picked Todd.

Will decides to follow through on his plan to photograph Casey and Todd secretly as they rendezvous at the boathouse each Saturday afternoon after golf. He is aware that Ally knows and finds the affair benign so she can officially obtain membership at the club. He had come across the handwritten note to Casey from Ally one night at Casey's house.

He's clever enough to know he can't use the angle of telling the wife about the affair, because it is a dead end. She already knows.

Will calls Casey one final time to review the status of their affair. He is displeased with how his social landscape is changing, and his hopes to recover his position at the boathouse and at the club with Casey consume him with desperate measures.

"I was planning to leave Olivia for you," Will tells Casey on the phone when she finally picks up. "You and I should be married, and I should be a member of SHCC with you." His voice almost sound crazy with determination. "I would do anything for you. You betrayed me with Todd at the boathouse already many times."

Casey answers him and tells him to go back to Olivia because their affair is over. Will is not satisfied with that.

"I have pictures of you and Todd at the boathouse taken by the boathouse boys numerous times. I don't think membership will do well when people realize that new members' husbands have to sleep with you to get in!" Will says angrily before hanging up the phone.

Will has a far more grand plan than just telling Ally. He is going to tell everyone about the club, which is far worse. They will all be ruined. Married men sleeping with board members to get in is quite a tale that the club would frown on. As he plots in his mind, Will looks at scrolls through pictures of Casey and Tom walking from the boathouse he took on his cell phone.

There is another plot to be had here with the membership committee at the club and those who wish to be granted official membership sleeping with board members. Even if their wives know it like Ally, this is a far larger scandal with potentially much larger consequences.

He surmises that the pictures can go to the local paper and to online sources, as well as to Casey's parents and the Palm Beach scene. It will be a scandal that will hit home at all country clubs and ruin Shore Haven Country Club and ruin Casey and Todd and all of them.

When the scandal breaks, no one will want to join the club. Wives won't want their husbands sleeping with the beautiful, seductive club president to get in. It will be public humiliation not just for Casey and Todd, but for the club.

"And Rich won't have a chance either," Will says, laughing to himself. He knows Rich has his own motivations to accept Todd and Casey's fling so he can move up on the board and be president someday.

It will damage all new and future memberships if the scandal breaks locally that husbands have to sleep with board members to gain membership to this exclusive club. No wife will want to sign up for that.

Will decides that unless someone pays his price financially, he is going to release the story to the local paper immediately. The only one who would benefit is Rich Hunter by possibly becoming president sooner after Casey is ousted. But without new membership, his tenure would be misguided, and he will soon realize that.

One afternoon, Will meets with Olivia, Rich, Tori, Todd, and Ally for drinks at the local restaurant-bar. Casey is not there for a reason. She will be filled in with this mess later on by Todd and can't be bothered to see Will in person again, especially in front of Ally now.

Olivia knows about the affair with Casey and has for a long time, so this is not new news to her, although it is public acknowledgement and a bit of a social disgrace as she silently admits she allowed it for social gain with invitations and club time as suspected. In this group, nobody's morals are sparkling white or clean enough to care about Olivia's morals.

In fact, the moral compass of this group is so far off that it is a nonissue.

Olivia just has to face the rest of them and share her awareness publically. She agrees to attend the meeting to gain details to help her sort out the mess and redirect her purpose. She can't lose Will to Casey or to the scandal.

Later that day, Olivia and Casey have to work on the benefit details together. They have to stuff invitations, which will be more mundane and annoying to Casey than any of this.

After they are all gathered, it does not take Will long to get to the point.

"I am going to the press with this story, and I have pictures of Todd and Casey from many events," Will says angrily, showing the pictures to Ally in front of Todd.

"You can't prove anything," Ally says while looking at the pictures. "It is just Casey and Todd walking from the boathouse at dusk." Her words are meant to support and protect her membership aspirations probably more than her marital bond.

"I can prove it with other explicit pictures you don't see here that the boat boys took for me many nights." As Will speaks, he angrily looks at Todd.

Ally knows the nature of pictures like this in an affair such as Casey and Todd's. She is not shocked in front of Todd and provides a united front. She and Todd had discussed the affair at home when she realized Will was going to call this illicit meeting. They are both on board.

Will is openly dismayed about the Bennets' united front, knowing it further hurts his chances of time with Casey again if Ally won't reel Todd home.

Ally accepts the affair, knowing membership will be secure. She also remembers the note she wrote about the green light to Casey and hopes that was securely fastened and battened down somewhere. She never knew what happened to that and questioned Bridgette's suggestion of handwriting it in the back of her mind.

Will may or may not have the pictures. All parties present assume he does. In his desperate state to protect his social status and resume relations with Casey, he would go to most lengths to accomplish what he wants.

He is becoming flustered by the fact that everyone is united against him, flustered that time with Casey may not happen, flustered that their agendas supersede his and diminish his importance at the club. More importantly, it diminishes his importance with Casey.

Most people know that Will always carries a revolver in the glove compartment of his Porsche. Todd looks him over head to toe to be sure he had left it in the car in his enraged state. It appears he had left it, thankfully. Will is a wild card at the club and at events, and that is one reason Casey was initially attracted to him. It is also one reason why Will and Olivia were never sponsored as members either.

"You are all going to contribute to me at least three months of your Wall Street salaries and your bonuses this year and next. If not, these picture go to newspaper and the story breaks. The story of married women giving up their husbands to the membership board to get in at club." Will details his plan quietly at the table.

"Out of the question," Rich says right away, affirming that choice with Tori, who looks pensive and scared. "That's too high a price for me, and you can't blackmail us!"

Todd and Ally nod in agreement.

"How can you prove that Ally knew anyhow?" Tori asks heatedly and directly. She nervously sips her white wine and appears somewhat concerned for the club and their futures. She realized that if the story breaks and membership drops, it will surely ruin her chances for being a wife of a club president someday also for sure.

"I intercepted a note that Ally left for Bridgette talking about green-lighting the project at Casey's. It was on her bureau, Todd. The note clearly shows Ally giving Casey the green light to go after Todd to get into the club." Will speaks with astute flair.

"Maybe we have been checkmated here after all," Todd notes. He looks at Ally without blame. Todd is pleased with the consolation prize of Ally's maneuvers at the club. He had achieved Casey's affections for the time being, and his wife openly supported it to get into the club. His life is succinctly punctuated.

He never assumed Ally would ever compromise him to get into the club. She hadn't seemed that socially calculating until now, which diminishes any romance that was left in their partnership. Todd is pleased that he found obvious lust and excitement with Casey and tuned out what had become a business arrangement now with Ally.

"No, we have not, and don't listen to him," Olivia states emphatically after taking in the discussion and reviewing the reactions. "There are other options, and Will can't force you to decide now right here."

Will gives Olivia angry stares to silence her.

"I have to go anyhow to the benefit meeting to stuff invites with none other than Casey next," Olivia quips, looking at Ally and Tori to see if they will come. They opt out. "Let's all go home and think about our options and report back to Will." Olivia gives a jubilant smile. She has already plotted option number two for herself while taking the meeting in.

If the pictures and story break, Olivia will be in social ruin with possible divorce, no club time, and social death and exclusion. With Will unfaithful publically, he will be cast in the list with Todd. She cannot deal with the public humiliation and will never be a member after this. Plus, it would tarnish any reputation she has ever established through her shallow ways. She knows she has to stop Will and had just concocted a plot to do so herself at the meeting.

Olivia is as shallow as the water off the boathouse dock in a sense but is quiet about it. She will never be as deep as the channel where the boats set sail at Shore Haven Country Club, but she knows how to navigate stormy weather well and is very clever at whatever she sets out to do.

Gossip is one thing. Print is another. Both are socially deadly. This is a social complication for Olivia, and she will accelerate a solution.

"I have a plan for Casey of all people," Olivia says to herself with a smile as she heads off to the church library to stuff invitations with Casey herself that afternoon.

The rest agree to go home that night after the restaurant meeting. Most take a weary and nervous feeling of their aspirations and plans with them as well.

Ally says to Todd, "Let's go meet with Bridgette and Drew at their house tonight for drinks." She starts to call them to let them know they are coming by.

Todd agrees and says, "Yes, they might be able to tell us what to do next."

Todd and Ally meet with Bridgette and Drew privately for advice at their house to sort through the scandal. The couple advises Ally and

Todd to pay the price for their actions financially with Will and agree to the blackmail.

Bridgette and Drew Mason have their own motivations and agendas. They both know that if the story breaks, the church will suffer morally and financially because of the scandal.

Initially, Bridgette had prompted Ally to green-light the Todd project with Casey. Drew was privy to the details and the players. Once it all came to fruition, it would be clear that they are just as hollow and blank as the church after service let out on Sunday. If that note were ever found, Bridgette would be ruined too if Ally broke her silence about that. Waters had to be tread carefully, even by the Masons, in this complex social group.

Bridgette was right; all relationships do need compromise, but to a point where there should be a red light or yellow to proceed with caution. The green light, all the green money, and all the green grass were just par for the proverbial course in Shore Haven Country Club and the landscape surrounding it.

CHAPTER 13

Role Reversal and Invites

Olivia is not as nonchalant about life in Shore Haven as she may appear under her sophisticated creamy skin as she's invited to all events in the area and at the clubs. She is not as subdued and uncalculating as she may appear. Rather, she is as clever and as stealth as Will for her own motivations.

Stuffing invites with Casey later, Olivia works out a secret plan of financial and social reward with her directly. Casey has more money than all the other players and is willing to part with it. She is just as willing to part with her money as she is to part with Will.

"I will take Will and the scandal away from Shore Haven for a price," Olivia tells Casey as she stuffs the endless, monotonous plethora of event invitations. She wonders why it is so posthumous to be on the committee to do clerical work anyhow. Casey feels the same way, although they never share it.

"Take Will away and never come back here to Shore Haven. Destroy whatever evidence he has, and the deal is done," Casey affirms, never looking Olivia directly in the eyes.

"Get us into Highland Shores Country Club with your connections and funds," Olivia negotiates. "Plus, my fee, of course." A ruthless victorious grin takes over her delicate face. She now has the final say with Casey now, and it's in her control now socially.

"Consider this done," Casey states, acknowledging that Olivia is in charge of the demands. She realizes that once Olivia and Will are gone, things will be back to normal. This was only momentary, and she collapsed to the social pressure and did what she had to do for herself and the club.

For Olivia, it is a lower price than Will initially sought financially, but it includes social control over Casey for the moment. It also comes with a new country club for the Hendrickses to be official members in. Casey demands personally that Will leave Shore Haven with the scandal permanently and agrees to Olivia's terms.

Sending Will off to social banishment in Highland Shores seems like a good solution. The consequences for all are too great if he stays local. There are social tremors that could go all the way to Palm Beach. For once, Olivia is in control of the situation socially; much to Casey's momentary chagrin, the roles had reversed.

After destroying all the evidence later that night, Olivia tells Will how it now stands and what she negotiated. His hand are tied like a sailor's figure eight knot at the boathouse. Will and Casey will end any ties with Shore Haven Country Club and the socialites. That is more for Olivia's ego. They also now have financial backing. Olivia explains that it is a win-win.

Will decides to end this subterfuge and agrees rather quickly to Olivia's surprise. They take the payoff quietly walk away to Highland Shores. Olivia is also happy to have Will to herself, and over at the posh club in Highland Shores, she will be perceived to have obtained her social goals finally.

They will be the new game in town over in Highland Shores and have money of substance and sustenance this time. It is their new social campus and playground. Unless, there is something else Will wants back in Shore Haven.

Will agrees to move to Highland Shores. After all, he received a nice financial sum, and Olivia had taken control of Casey, which impressed him.

In Highland Shores, it will seem less obvious when he stakes out Casey's boathouse rendezvous at the club back in Shore Haven. However, being removed from Shore Haven only angers him more. His jealousy is heightened even though his bank account is full. Todd gets to stay close to Casey Tate and Will does not, and Will still loves her madly.

CHAPTER 14

The Next Wave

*M*ost of the dust settles at the club after Will and Olivia Hendricks leave for Highland Shores. All seems just about back to normal at the club, and everyone takes a voluminous proverbial breather, knowing the scandal is silenced.

Though Casey Tate had to offer up a financial sum, it was worth saving herself and the club. The Bennets were approved as official members when the committee met.

Ally is significantly relieved, although she still medicates openly with shopping, alcohol, and professional therapy. She prefers the business relationship she and Todd have acquired to achieve their social goals. Casey is fickle and will drop Todd soon, just as she dropped Will, Ally rationalizes often.

"So glad we finally got in," Ally says to Todd as they sit by the fire inside the clubhouse together for show. She does not really mind the social or sexual compromises she had to make to achieve her social goals. She figures it will all sort out in time.

"It is what you wanted," Todd answers quickly, looking at his watch. "I'm having a drink with Rich to thank him and celebrate." Todd gets up and walks off toward the grill room to find Rich and talk to him briefly about another issue.

"Casey's pregnant," Todd confides to Rich. "She told me this morning just after we got into the club officially." As he speaks, Todd's eyes are fixed on his beer.

"Wow. She works fast. She just set me up in line to be president next. Is she going to have the baby? Membership is going to drop for sure after this breaks. What about Ally?" Rich questions.

He is concerned for Todd but more concerned for himself and the club. "Tori only stayed with me hoping one day I'd be club president. I have known that for years. She will probably divorce me now." Rich sighs.

As Rich pauses to think about things, he realizes it would be somewhat of a relief to be divorced from Tori's expensive expenditures. Maybe after, then he could really focus on golf. Maybe he'd meet another younger woman like Todd and start over. Tori is as disposable to him as he was to her.

"Casey told me she is going to have the baby. So, Ally and I are in the same boat with divorce looming, I suspect," Todd says, wondering if Casey and he will get married. He had already emotionally left Ally long ago when he found out she had used him to strategize getting into the club. It's now just a blank and shattered business partnership.

The news of Casey's pregnancy will not shatter his marriage to Ally. That was already shattered. However, it could serve as proof of the scandal. If Will talks, the truth will be told.

Casey is going to have the baby either way because it is her final trophy of the affair. Plus, she wants Will to find out about it as an added punctuation of her disdain for him.

Having the baby compromises the club, but it accentuates to Will that he is out of Shore Haven forever and his ludicrous advances must be over. Casey is pleased with that detail and her strategy.

The scandal of Casey's baby will stain the club even worse than the story Will planned to release. The baby is all the living, literal proof anyone needs of someone one the membership committee sleeping with the husband of a sponsored family.

"I can't enrage Will any further by news of our baby, Todd," Casey says nervously over dinner at her house. "He is still calling me and wants me back and is enraged that he is in Highland Shores, which he considers social Siberia." Casey quips. She is losing social control of everything now in her previously solidly managed club world.

"Bridgette asked me not to come to church on Sundays until the baby is born because people are talking, and it is hurting their Sunday membership," Casey says with annoyance. "Can you believe she would say that to me?"

"Well, it is a scandal of sorts still. I am just getting divorced on top of it too and hopefully marrying you," Todd says with a questioning look in his eyes. He certainly wants to marry Casey and diffuse the scandal for the club and themselves somewhat.

"Members are all talking about membership committees and us apparently and the club everywhere," Casey says with a worried look. "I hope Will has not found out about the baby, because he will be even more upset. It would seal his fate to never have me, and he might go to desperate measures. His calls have been beyond upsetting lately."

About this time, Bridgette and Drew see a decline in worshipers and faith and members on Sundays too. Drew and Bridgette worry that in a few months, they will be replaced at church if membership falls off and there are financial strains at the church. They don't want to move again to some less socially important and elite church elsewhere.

Stories in the newspaper may get tossed out in next week's garbage, but gossip seems to stick like champagne on the floor that's been spilled at a party. The news of Casey's baby would stick for a long time in Shore Haven.

"I don't think Will is aware of things here, and he has not been spotted at the club or in Shore Haven lately," Todd assures her. He had already asked club security to note if Will's car shows up unannounced or if he's spotted about in town.

"Well, in Shore Haven you are either in or out. No one from here talks to the Hendrickses now, or the Masons. They are all pretty much socially disposable to me anyhow," Casey reminds herself, feeling comforted and regaining more control of the social landscape.

Todd answers with a reassuring smile. "There's the Casey I know. The one who is confident and in control of every aspect."

"Will just makes me nervous at times because he is sort of erratic and not centered," Casey notes.

The news has not, in fact, reached Highland Shores or Will and Olivia. Hardly anyone who's anyone kept contact with the Hendrickses once they moved. Casey is right. That is the way Shore Haven operates. You are either in or out. The Hendrickses are out with a lot of people over in Shore Haven and were never really in. They always knew they were easily socially disposable.

Casey couldn't care less about anything in Highland Shores anyhow and wants Will to stay far away from her over there. She has a new role at the club it seems. She is going be the mother of Todd's baby and his wife down the road if she chooses to be for social reasons after his divorce. At least it is not Will she's contemplating marrying under these circumstances.

CHAPTER 15

The Boathouse after Dark

Even though Will had been removed to Highland Shores Country Club, he returned regularly, secretly avoiding club security. After dark in his midnight-navy Porsche, Will still comes to Shore Haven Country Club unannounced and unknown to anyone.

He arrives after dark to watch what continues on at the boathouse with Todd and Casey. Will is still unaware of the detail of the pregnancy. He is still so jealous of Todd, and he watches them come and go as he tries to devise a plan to win Casey back. Watching them just fuels his jealousy and increases his urge to settle the score with Todd somehow.

He had been witnessing the trysts at the boathouse from the parking lot up on the hill for months, and it just fueled his fire and anger. When Will was at the boathouse, he recalled those times as pinnacle lovemaking. He cannot get her off his mind. He loves her and wants her back, and it was destroying him that Todd has her now.

He despises Highland Shores and having to start all over again socially to top it off. It enrages him as much as being isolated from Casey, as much as being jealous of Todd for having Casey. Highland Shores is like social Siberia to Will. Coming back to Shore Haven with Casey would be the solution, and Todd had to be removed from this landscape.

Will is desperate to get Casey back into his life and come back to Shore Haven Country Club with her. There is nothing in writing regarding the payoff with Olivia. He can proceed as he wishes for his own desires.

His rage was silent, and his betrayal was as deep as the water near the dock at the boathouse at Shore Haven Country Club. The same boathouse that he once enjoyed for his afternoon and sunset romps with Casey Tate. Before Todd arrived onshore.

After Casey departs into the clubhouse this particular evening, Will decides it is time to resolve the situation with Todd. Casey goes inside quickly because she is feeling somewhat ill during the early stages of her pregnancy. She is chilled and goes to get a warm blanket inside and wait for Todd by the fire. Todd stays outside to finish his cocktail and look at the boats still in the water.

Will sees Casey leave. He shines his headlights down toward the boathouse in an attempt to see if Todd is down there by himself. He leaves the lights on as he slowly walks down the hill toward the boathouse in his navy blazer and a scarf around his neck dangling unevenly to one side. It is dark, and the air is crisp, as crisp as the plan he has to confront Todd now.

In case anything happens, Will takes the revolver out of his glove compartment and puts it in his blazer pocket. He comes upon Todd, who stands there taking in the sound of the water on this cool, crisp night. He is also attired in his wool blazer and holding his gin and tonic with ice.

Todd turns as he hears something behind him. He thinks he hears the rustle of the leaves and looks to see if it is Casey returning to the dock. He had told her to meet him inside by the fire in the clubhouse. It was ok for them to be seen around the club together now.

Today, Todd had told Ally about Casey and the baby and their divorce was imminent. Everything was out in the open fall air. He had just been listening to the clinking of the ice in his glass and comparing it to the ebb and flow of the tide hitting the dock to settle his mind about all the matters at hand.

He turns to see Will instead in the darkness. Will is standing there in the cold air with a dark look in his distant icy, eyes. Todd looks at him with the car lights still aimed down toward them from Will's car on the hill. They are two big, round headlights beaming down toward the boathouse.

In a fluster of nervous, cold jealous, Will says, "She's always been for me, Todd. You got in the way of Shore Haven Country Club and my world with Casey."

"Will, you are not supposed to be here at the club anymore," Todd reminds him.

Those words enrage Will to another degree because Todd has gained more control as an actual member now.

"Casey's pregnant now anyhow, Will. It's truly time for you to move on," Todd says.

"Pregnant? With your baby?" Will's rage heightens in his eyes. It should be his baby not Todd's in his mind.

"Yes, it is mine," Todd says affirmatively, taking one last sip of his gin and tonic and putting the glass down.

Todd turns his back to look out and take in all the sounds and lights over the water. Turning to Will, Todd says, "You never really could have her now anyhow, Will. You were never going to be a member here. You know that," Todd states arrogantly. He turns back to look at the water again with an air of accomplishment about getting Casey pregnant, which was something he never considered.

Hearing that comment causes Will to fume inside. He was going to be a member, if Todd hadn't come into the picture. Brutal thoughts immediately pulsate through Will's head in his fury.

Moments with Casey fragment his mind in bits and pieces. He imagines Casey with Todd in the boathouse, and his mind explodes with unscrupulous, undiffused anger.

Will removes his revolver from his coat pocket and aims it at the back of Todd's head as he stands looking out at the water. He pauses and looks back toward the grounds of the club to quickly verify that no one is there.

He fires one deadly shot into Todd's head and then stands silently as he watches him collapse face-first off the dock and into the cold water by the boathouse.

Will turns and leaves, quickly walking toward the headlights still on to guide him back to his getaway car as it now became. He tosses his revolver in the watery grave with Todd near the deep part of the channel.

Out on the lawn, in the glow from the headlights, he sees Casey running down toward the boathouse from the clubhouse with a blanket wrapped around her. She runs past Will and ignores him even in this desperate state as she sees him walking toward his car.

"You are not a member. Get out of here! You were never going to be a member, ever! I called security as soon as I saw your car!" Casey screams at Will in a hurried flurry as she runs past him, desperate to find Todd.

Will does not answer and keeps walking away, back toward his car.

Casey runs to the dock and discovers Todd alone in the grips water. She is devastated and jarred by the consequences of Will's actions and realizes her love for Todd was not just a tryst or social plot. She sits on the dock in deep despair, shattered with no resolution imminent, financially, morally, or socially.

All of the maneuvering and compromises at the Shore Haven Country Club seemed so entirely vapid now. Casey has no further depth left, and volumes of money can not relieve that plight. Their world was now to become magnanimous social scandal at Shore Haven Country Club of scandal and murder.

Because of this event, the club and their lives had just become a stale, tainted blank canvas with nothing socially left to paint. The brushes are stuck with old paint and old tales of what had happened that year on the membership committee and on the dock at the boathouse.

In a world of attaining social status and aspiring for more, members lost themselves and much more that was priceless. Fear and their misguided dreams allowed them to make social compromises.

These compromises were all red lights, or should have been, like the port side of the boats when they were all heading into port off the dock at the now-famous boathouse at the club. Shore Haven Country Club remains forever as tarnished as the golf and sailing trophies on display in the clubhouse, and nothing will ever alleviate that social humiliation or condition. The void at the club and in the club members lives will never be filled or satiated again. There was nothing left to socially seek.

Printed in the United States
By Bookmasters